THE BOY WHO FOUND THE LIGHT

The Boy
Who Found the Light

Eskimo folktales retold and illustrated with
wood engravings by Dale DeArmond

Sierra Club Books | **Little, Brown and Company**
SAN FRANCISCO | BOSTON TORONTO LONDON

The Sierra Club, founded in 1892 by John Muir, has devoted itself to the study and protection of the earth's scenic and ecological resources—mountains, wetlands, woodlands, wild shores and rivers, deserts and plains. The publishing program of the Sierra Club offers books to the public as a nonprofit educational service in the hope that they may enlarge the public's understanding of the Club's basic concerns. The Sierra Club has some sixty chapters in the United States and in Canada. For information about how you may participate in its programs to preserve wilderness and the quality of life, please address inquiries to Sierra Club, 730 Polk Street, San Francisco, CA 94109.

A YOLLA BOLLY PRESS BOOK

The Boy Who Found the Light was edited and prepared for publication at The Yolla Bolly Press, Covelo, California, under the supervision of James and Carolyn Robertson. Editorial and production staff: Nancy Campbell, Diana Fairbanks. Composition by Wilsted & Taylor, Oakland, California.

COPYRIGHT © 1990 BY DALE DE ARMOND

FIRST EDITION

LIBRARY OF CONGRESS CATALOGING-IN-PUBLICATION DATA

DeArmond, Dale.
    The boy who found the light : Eskimo folktales / retold and
illustrated with wood engravings by Dale DeArmond. — 1st ed.
       p.   cm.
    Summary: An illustrated collection of Eskimo folktales.
    ISBN 0-316-17787-3
    1. Eskimos—Legends. [1. Eskimos—Legends. 2. Indians of North
America—Legends.] I. Title.
    E99.E7D3453   1990
    398.2'089971—dc20   90-31271
                                              CIP
                                              AC

10 9 8 7 6 5 4 3 2 1

BP

Sierra Club Books/Little, Brown children's books are published by Little, Brown and Company (Inc.) in association with Sierra Club Books.

Printed in the United States of America

For Heather and E.B.

Contents

Glossary

Inua (ee-NEW-ah): Soul or spirit. Each living thing, in the Eskimo belief, has an inua that can take other forms.

Kashim (ka-SHEEM): Village meeting house.

Mukluks (MUCK-lucks): Sealskin boots.

Parka (PAR-kee): A hooded, coatlike, fur outer garment.

Ptarmigan (TAR-mi-gan): Game bird, brown in summer, white in winter. The official bird of Alaska.

Shaman (SHAW-man): Medicine man, witch doctor, conjuror.

Tulugac (too-LOO-gac): Raven.

Tundra (TUN-dra): The (almost) treeless arctic plain.

Yuguk (YOO-guk): Doll.

The Boy Who Found the Light

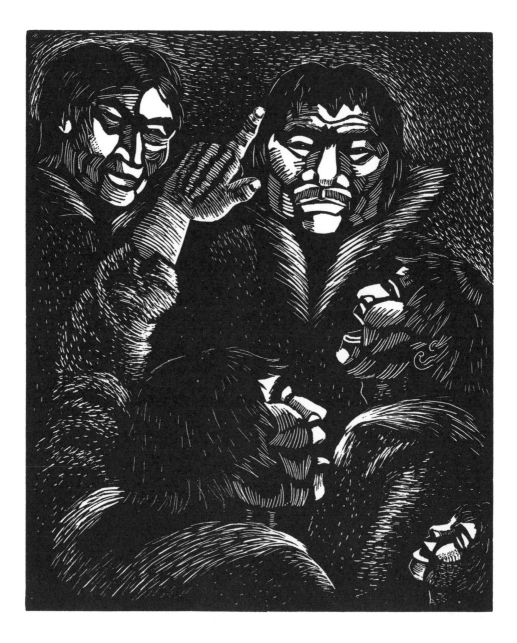

Long ago everything was dark.

There was no daylight at all. The oldest grandfathers in the village said that their grandfathers could remember that once the sun and the moon had hung in the sky and there had been light. But for as long as anyone could remember, there was only the dim light from the seal oil lamps that were kept burning in the little houses and in the kashim, the village meeting house, where the men gathered.

The men talked of hunting and where to find the best fishing places. They told old tales, and often the talk turned to the time when there had been light, and people could walk around and see everything, and the sun had been warm in the summer, and at night the moon hung in the sky. They wondered where the light had all gone, leaving only darkness.

In this same village there was a little orphan boy called Tulugac. His parents had gone out on the sea ice to hunt one day and had never returned. People in the village thought he was a little simple. They weren't unkind to him, and sometimes they remembered to give him a little food, or a village woman would notice how ragged he was and give him a worn parka her children had outgrown or a pair of old mukluks. But he was often cold and hungry. He was a brave and cheerful little boy, however, and made the best of what he had. At night he slept in a corner of the kashim, wrapped in a couple of old sleeping skins someone had thrown on the village trash heap.

When the old men talked about how warm it had been in the old days, when the sun had shone in the sky, Tulugac thought how wonderful it must have been. He wondered whether he could find the light and bring it back. Sometimes the old men talked about the moon. In one of the tales the moon hung in the sky at night, and each night you could see more of it, until you could see the whole round moon. Then it would grow smaller and smaller again. It sounded very beautiful in that old tale, and the child longed to see it.

Tulugac had one treasure. His mother had given him a little birdskin covered with shining black feathers, just before she disappeared on the ice. She had told him, "This is great magic and it will bring you good luck. Take good care of it and keep it with you always." Tulugac carried it under his clothes close to his heart, and it comforted him to feel it there.

Every now and then the shamans would meet in the kashim and try to bring back the light. They would cast their most

16

powerful spells and sing chants and dance until they fell down exhausted. And all the people would chant, and the drummers would drum, but nothing came of it. It was cold and dark, and it stayed cold and dark.

One night in the kashim two great shamans danced and sang and cast spells until they could hardly move. All the people chanted until they were hoarse. The drummers beat so hard on their drums that they broke them. Still nothing happened.

Tulugac, sitting in his corner and dreaming of the sun, said aloud, "I'll bet I can find the light."

Everybody in the kashim looked at him. They were astonished that this ragged little boy, who didn't even have good sense, would dare to think he could do something that even the greatest shamans couldn't do. They roared with laughter. But the shamans, who had worked so hard and used their most powerful magic without making even one little ray of light, were very angry.

One shaman grabbed the boy by the shoulder and said, "All right, if you know so much, you go and find the light. Don't come back until you bring the sun with you." And he threw Tulugac out into the snowy darkness.

Tulugac picked himself up and brushed off the snow. He wondered whatever had made him say such a thing out loud. Then suddenly he felt a faint stirring where the little birdskin lay against his skin, and he thought, "Maybe I *can* find the light and bring it back."

19

Tulugac's only relative in the village was an old aunt who had lived there as long as anyone could remember. People said she was a witch, and they were a little afraid of her. But she had always been kind to the boy and sometimes she gave him food, so he went to her house and told her what had happened.

Then he said, "Please, Auntie, tell me where the light is so I can go and bring it back."

"I don't know where the light is," said the old woman. "You were a very foolish boy to say you could do something that even the greatest shamans couldn't do."

"Auntie," said the boy, "you do know where the light is. I know you do because you couldn't have done such fine sewing on that beautiful parka you wear unless you had light to see. I must find the sun and the moon and bring them back. All the people need them."

Tulugac argued and pleaded, and at last the old woman gave in, saying, "I didn't want to tell you because it is very dangerous for you to go there. But I know you won't quit pestering me until you know. Here is what you must do to find the light: put on your boots and go to the south. It is a long, long journey and the way is dark and cold. You will know when you get to the right place. Should danger threaten you, put on the little birdskin your mother gave you. Or have you lost it? Boys are so careless."

"Of course I haven't lost it, Auntie," said Tulugac. "But it is only as big as my hand. How can I put it on?"

"Never you mind," said the old woman. "Just do as I say. Here is a bit of fat to eat along the way. Now off you go, big mouth boy, and good luck to you."

Tulugac tucked the bit of fat away inside his parka, put on an old pair of mukluks that someone had given him, and set off for the south. He traveled a long time in the cold and darkness. He became so tired he couldn't lift his feet one more time.

He dug a little cave in a snowbank and crawled into it, and pulled a block of snow across the entrance to shut out the wind. It was bitter cold, but the little birdskin seemed to give off warmth. Tulugac fell asleep and dreamed of walking on the sunlit tundra. Little plants and flowers grew on the tundra, and there were berries to eat. When he awoke he found that a small hare had crept into his snow cave and curled up against him for warmth. The hare would have fled in terror when Tulugac awoke, but the boy said, "Don't be afraid, little sister. I won't harm you."

"Thank you, big one," said the hare. "What are you doing out here in the cold and dark so far from your village?"

"I seek the light," said Tulugac. "Can you tell me if this is the way?"

"This is the way," said the hare. "But it is far to the south from here. Good luck to you." And away she hopped.

After the hare had gone, Tulugac ate some of the fat his aunt had given him, and set out once more to the south. He traveled for many hours, and, when he was so weary he could go no farther, he dug another snow cave and crept into it. He ate some

more of the fat, which never seemed to get any smaller. Then he fell asleep and dreamed again of the summer world.

And so it went for many days and nights. He walked until he was too tired to go farther, then slept in a snow cave. The dream stayed with him and gave him courage.

One day, as he trudged along and wondered whether he would ever reach the light or would just go on forever through the cold and dark, Tulugac walked right into a big mother bear. He was so frightened his heart almost stopped. He was sure the bear would tear him to pieces and eat him on the spot. But the bear put out her great paw and said, "Wait, little brother. I won't harm you.

You are one of us, you know. But what are you doing out here alone in the cold and dark?"

"I seek the light, mother bear," said Tulugac, his voice still shaky with fear. "Can you tell me if this is the way?"

"This is the way," said the bear. "Come, I will travel with you for a piece of the trail, and we can keep each other company." All that day the bear traveled with Tulugac and told him stories that bear mothers tell their cubs in the winter dens. When the boy stumbled with weariness, she let him ride on her great, broad back.

At last the bear said, "Here I must leave you. My den is near, and it is almost time for me to birth my cubs and sleep. Good luck to you, little brother."

Tulugac was sorry to leave the bear, but on he went, sleeping in snow caves when he was tired and nibbling his bit of fat when he was hungry. He was lonely and tired of this traveling on and on. Often he thought it would be much better to be back in his dim corner of the kashim, listening to the men talk, even if he was often cold and hungry.

Once, as he traveled along grumbling to himself that he was stupid to have ever started on this miserable journey, he felt something brush against him, and was so startled he cried out.

"Hush, little brother," said a great snowy owl, who had come out of the darkness on her silent wings, as snowy owls do. "Where are you off to? You should be home in your village, not out here wandering alone in the dark."

"I seek the light," said Tulugac. "I told the shamans I could find it, and I really thought I could. But now that I've traveled so long, I'm just not sure anymore. Tell me, mother owl, is this the way?"

"This is the way, little brother. Have courage and keep going." And off she flew as silently as falling snow.

So Tulugac continued on his way, feeling more and more lost and lonely. One day, when he had almost lost heart, he felt the little birdskin stir and flutter, and the next moment he thought he saw a ray of light. When he looked harder, it disappeared, but then he saw it again, brighter than before.

Tulugac was so excited he forgot he was tired. He began to hurry toward the light. Sometimes it was very bright. Then it would disappear, and all would be black again. At last he could make out a great hill, very bright on one side and dark as night on the other. Close against the hill stood a hut, and in front of the hut an enormous old man was shoveling snow, throwing the snow so high it completely shut out the light.

Tulugac crept closer, and at last he could see the light he had come so far to find. It was so bright he could hardly bear to look at it, and it seemed to be a great ball of fire. A smaller, dimmer light floated close by. He tried to think how he could get them.

The little birdskin fluttered, and Tulugac took courage and walked boldly up to the old man. He said, "Why do you throw the snow and hide the light? There has been no light in my village for many years."

27

The old man stopped shoveling and said, "I'm not trying to hide the light. I'm just shoveling the snow away from my doorway. But who are you, and why do you come here?"

"I'm Tulugac," said the boy. "It is always dark in our village, and I don't like it. I've come to live with you."

"What? Do you mean all the time?" the old man asked.

"Yes," said Tulugac. "All the time."

"That is well," said the old man. "Come into the house." He dropped his shovel on the ground near the light. Stooping, he led the way into the underground passage to the house. He let the bearskin curtain drop as he entered, thinking the boy was right behind him.

The moment the door flap fell, Tulugac seized the smaller ball of light, the moon, and hurled it into the sky. To this day it still turns round and round from the force of Tulugac's throwing arm. That is why we sometimes see only the thin edge of its light, and then as it turns we see the full face.

After he had hurled the moon into the sky, Tulugac tucked the larger light under his arm, took the old man's shovel in his other hand, and set off running as fast as he could go. It was only a moment before the old man realized what had happened. He set out after the boy, and Tulugac could hear his frightful roars and shrieks of rage as he grew closer and closer.

Just as the old man's hands were about to close upon him, Tulugac remembered his aunt's words. He snatched out the little birdskin, which immediately surrounded him. Tulugac became a raven flying swiftly and smoothly through the air. When the old man saw that Tulugac had become a raven and was leaving him behind, he cried out, "You may keep the light, but let me have my shovel."

"No," said the raven-boy. "You made our village dark for many years, and you can't have your shovel. I am going to drop it in the ocean."

When the old man heard that, he went into such a rage that he flew into a thousand pieces, and no one ever saw him again.

As Tulugac, the raven, flew north toward his home, he broke off a piece of the light and threw it away so there was daylight everywhere. How wonderful it was to see the beautiful earth at last. Mountains and rivers and tundra and ocean spread out before him.

When it grew dark again he flew awhile without throwing out any more light. Then he broke off another piece and threw it out. Sometimes he waited a long time before he threw out another piece of light, and that is why we have the long nights of winter. Sometimes he threw out more light very soon, making the short nights and long days of summer.

When the raven-boy reached his home village he threw out the last piece of light. Then he became the little orphan boy, Tulugac, again. All the people of the village came running when the light burst upon them. Tulugac said, "There, you great shamans, I have brought back the light. The sun and the moon will hang in the sky, and it will be light and then dark so that

there will be day and night, always and forever." And so it is to this day.

Then Tulugac went out on the sea ice. After a while there was a great storm, and the ice broke away and floated to the other shore. Tulugac walked along the shore until he came to a fine, big village. The people of the village made him welcome, and he stayed there and became a great hunter. And whatever he did and wherever he went, he carried the little birdskin next to his heart.

After a time Tulugac married a young woman from the village, and they had three daughters and four sons.

When Tulugac was an old man he called his children to him and told them how he had come to this country. He bade them return to their father's country, and he gave each of the children a shining feather from the little birdskin. Then he died.

After Tulugac's death his children did as he told them to do. They returned to their father's country, and there they became ravens. They could still become people when they wished to, but after a while their descendents forgot how to change themselves into people, and so they are ravens to this day.

The Raven and the Marmot

One beautiful, bright spring morning

a raven was flying along the shore feeling well-pleased with himself and the world. He was keeping one eye out for food, as he generally does, and he came upon a flock of sea birds. The sea birds immediately began to tease him, calling out, "Here comes the carrion-eater!" and "Let's chase the dirty, black thing away." And they all flew after him, yelling, "Raven eats carrion! Raven eats dead things!"

The raven was much put out by this. He thinks very well of himself, and expects others to do the same. To escape his tormentors he flew inland toward the mountains, muttering, "Gnak-gnak-gnak. Why are those stupid birds saying such things of me? I've done them no harm," but quite forgetting the times he had sneaked into their nests and eaten their eggs.

When he was well away from the sea birds, the raven landed in a small mountain meadow. He saw a marmot hole close by, and, always curious about other people's business, he moved even closer and stood there watching the hole. Soon the marmot, who had been out gathering food for his winter store, came back. He saw the raven there and said politely, "Good day to you, Raven. Would you step aside, please, so I can go into my burrow?"

"No, I won't step aside," said the raven. "The sea birds called me carrion-eater, and I'll show them that I am not. I'm going to eat you right here on the spot."

The marmot was terribly alarmed, but he was a quick-thinking little marmot, so he said, "Very well, Raven, eat me if you must. But please grant me one favor before I meet my end. I've always heard that you are a wonderful dancer, and I would really like to see such a fine sight before I go."

The raven was very flattered by this and said grandly, "Ah, yes, Marmot, I'll be very happy to give you the pleasure of seeing me dance, which I do very well, if I may say so. Sing, Marmot, and I will dance."

So the marmot sang:

Oh, Raven, great Raven,
How gracefully you dance,
With lifted foot and fluttering wing
It's the finest dance I've ever seen.

And the raven capered clumsily about.

At last they both stopped to rest, and the marmot said, "Ah, Raven, what a truly magnificent sight. I will die happy if you will close your eyes and dance for me just one more time."

"Very well," said the raven, quite enchanted with this praise. "I can't deny you the pleasure. Sing, Marmot." And he closed his eyes and began solemnly hopping from one foot to the other while the marmot sang:

Oh, Raven, great Raven,
How gracefully you dance.
With lifted foot and fluttering wing,
You're the biggest fool I've ever seen!

41

And with the last words the marmot darted past the raven and safely into his burrow. He stuck out his head and laughed and laughed. "Chi-kik-kik-kik. Raven, if you could only see how silly you looked hopping about like that. I could hardly sing for laughing at you. And now you don't get to eat me after all. Just look how fat I am. Aren't you sorry you can't have me for your dinner? Chi-kik-kik-kik."

The raven was so angry and disgusted that he flew off without another word.

The Doll

One winter night a long time ago,

a man and his wife sat talking. The woman was sewing a pair of
mukluks for her husband, and the man was carving a piece of
ivory to carry with him and bring him good luck.

"Husband," said the woman, "why do you suppose we have
no children when all our neighbors in the village have two or
three? I do not understand it."

"Neither do I," said the man. "It's just the way things are, I
guess. It's too bad. I would like to have a child in the house."

The wife sighed, and then she said, "Since we have no children

I want you to go out on the tundra to where a solitary little tree grows. Bring back a part of the trunk and carve a doll from it."

"Now what sort of nonsense is that?" asked the man. "Dolls are for children. What good will it be?"

"Please, husband, do as I ask," said the woman. "I had a dream, and that is how I know the tree is there. The tree spoke to me and said you should carve a doll from its trunk."

The husband grumbled a bit, but he was a kind man. He could see that his wife had her heart set on having a doll, so he put on his snowshoes and set off.

When he reached the edge of the village, he saw a track of bright light. He followed the track of light for a long way, and at last he could see a shining object far ahead. When he came close he saw that it was indeed a small tree, glittering and gleaming like a million snow crystals. The man was a little afraid of the magical tree, but it seemed to beckon to him. Calling upon all his courage, he hurriedly cut a piece of the trunk of the tree and went home with it.

When he reached home he sat down and began at once to carve a doll from the piece of wood. He was a skilled carver, and the wood seemed almost to shape itself in his hands. Before long he presented his wife with a beautiful image of a little boy.

The wife was delighted with her doll, and set to work at once to make parkas and britches and mukluks for it.

While she worked she said to her husband, "Our dishes are too big for the doll. Please make some toy dishes for him."

46

"Oh, come now," said the man. "Toy dishes indeed! What's the use of all this?"

"It will give us something to talk about besides ourselves. The doll will give us amusement and conversation, and it will seem much more real if the doll has its own little dishes," coaxed the woman.

"Oh, very well," said the man, who really did like to carve and was quite pleased with the little doll he had made. Without any more argument he carved a set of toy dishes.

When all was finished, the wife dressed the doll and set it in the place of honor opposite the entrance to the house. She put food and water in front of it in the toy dishes. Then the couple went to bed.

Sometime in the night the woman was awakened by low whistling sounds. She shook her husband to wake him and said, "Listen! That must be the doll."

"It can't be," said the husband. "It's only a wooden figure. You hear a mouse."

"No," said the wife, "it's the doll. I can tell." And when she made a light she could see that the food and water were gone, and she was sure the doll's eyes moved.

She was delighted. She picked up the doll and held it and played with it as though it were a real child. It seemed to her the little figure responded and became less wooden in her arms. "See, husband," she said, "he is getting real."

The man still thought she was imagining things and that a

48

mouse had eaten the food and drunk the water, but his wife was so happy that he said nothing.

When the woman grew tired, she tenderly placed the doll beside her and went to sleep. When they awoke in the morning, even the husband could see that the doll was changing. All that

49

day the woman held the doll and talked to it whenever she had time from her household tasks. She called the doll "Yuguk," and kept it by her while she prepared the food and worked at her skin sewing. When she and her husband ate she put food and water before the little figure, and, though neither of them saw the doll eat or drink, the food and water were always gone when they looked again.

By the next morning it was plain to see that Yuguk was becoming a real little boy. Little by little as that day passed he became a human child.

Yuguk was a happy, cheerful little boy, and gave his parents much pleasure. The only strange thing about him was his eyes. They were very bright and almost seemed to give off light.

When the other villagers asked about him, the couple said that Yuguk was their nephew and had come to live with them. Before long, they almost forgot how strangely Yuguk had come to them, and thought of him as their real son.

Yuguk played with the other village children and ran and shouted like any other child, except that he could run faster than anyone in the village. He could always win the races, but he was so good-natured that he often let another child win.

One day Yuguk said to his father, "Please, Father, make me a strong, sharp knife." And he said to his mother, "Please, Mother, make me some warm clothes, for I must go on a long journey and it will be very cold."

His parents were curious and a little alarmed, and begged the boy to tell them where he was going. Yuguk was reluctant to talk about it but at last he said, "I only know I must follow the shining path. When I get to the right place, I will know what I have to do."

The man and his wife remembered the shining path and how Yuguk had come to them so many years before. They were sad that Yuguk must leave them, but the boy promised he would return when he had finished his task.

His father made him a strong, sharp knife, and his mother made a beautiful warm parka sewed with the very finest stitches. She also made britches and warm mukluks and grass socks to wear inside the mukluks.

When all was ready Yuguk put on his warm clothes, took his sharp knife, thanked his parents for all they had done for him, and told them goodbye.

As soon as Yuguk was outside the village he saw the shining path his father had followed to the magical tree. Running lightly and swiftly, Yuguk followed the bright path. Sometimes he stopped to rest and sleep, and then he was off again. At last he reached the edge of day where the sky comes down and walls in the daylight. To the east, close to where the path led him, he could see a place were there was a gutskin cover over a hole in the sky wall. The cover bulged as though a great force were pushing on it.

Yuguk looked about him and said, "It's very quiet here. I think

a little wind will make things better." He pulled out his knife and cut the cover away from the hole. At once a great wind rushed through, bringing with it trees and bushes and now and then a live caribou.

Yuguk looked through the hole he had opened and saw that there was another world just like the earth on the other side of the sky wall. Then he closed and fastened the gutskin cover. He said to the wind, "Blow hard sometimes, blow light sometimes, and sometimes do not blow at all."

Then Yuguk went on along the shining path, staying close to the sky wall. To the southeast he found another gutskin-covered hole. When he cut the cover loose a great gale blew through, bringing with it grasses and flowers, live geese and ptarmigan. "That is good," said Yuguk. "The hunters will like those too." He commanded the southeast wind as he had the other, "Blow hard sometimes, blow light sometimes, and sometimes do not blow at all."

By this time Yuguk was tired. He found a sheltered place against the sky wall, ate a bit of the food his mother had given him for the journey, and curled up and went to sleep.

When he woke in the morning Yuguk went on along the sky wall. He saw that on the earth plain the caribou had increased during the night, and now a great herd of them was running around the tundra. Overhead a flock of geese went by, and the ptarmigan were calling in the bushes.

Yuguk continued to the south along the shining path. After

a while he came to another bulging hole in the sky wall, and when he put his hand on it, it felt warm. He cut away the gut-skin cover, and a warm wind rushed in, bringing rain and spray from the great ocean on the other side of the sky wall. With the spray came seals and a great whale. Yuguk quickly closed the hole and commanded the south wind as he had the others, "Blow hard sometimes, blow light sometimes, and sometimes do not blow at all."

Yuguk rested then and ate some food and slept. When he started out again he traveled to the west, and after a long time he came to another opening in the sky wall. When he cut the cover loose, the west wind brought a heavy rainstorm and sleet and spray from the ocean. Two great walrus came tumbling through the hole before Yuguk could replace the cover. He instructed the west wind as he had the others, "Blow hard sometimes, blow light sometimes, and sometimes do not blow at all."

As he went farther along the sky wall, it got colder and colder, and the Milky Way rang beneath his feet and glittered and shone. The cold was so bitter that he could no longer bear it close to the sky wall, so he made a circuit until he saw another opening. He hesitated and then cut away the cover, letting in a terrifying blast of ice and snow that strewed itself over the earth plain, and the north wind entered the world, bringing with it two great white bears.

Yuguk was instantly chilled to the bone. Half frozen, he struggled to replace the cover. Still gasping with the cold, he told the north wind as he had the others, "Blow hard sometimes, blow light sometimes, and sometimes do not blow at all."

After he had closed the hole, Yuguk saw that there were no others, and he started toward the middle of the earth plain. When he reached the very center of the earth plain, he looked to the sky and saw that it was held up by many long slender poles arranged like the poles in a tepee. The poles were made of pale, shining light.

Yuguk gazed in wonder at the splendor of the sky and the Milky Way where he had traveled so far. Then he turned and made his way toward his home.

When he reached the village Yuguk made a circle around it, visiting each house and asking all the people to gather in the kashim. When everyone had come into the kashim Yuguk told them how they were to hunt the animals that had come through the sky wall with the winds. He warned them that they must never kill for sport, but only for the meat they needed, and that meat must never be wasted. He taught the people that animals are just like people, and must be treated with respect. And he taught them that they should make masks and pay honor to the inuas, spirits, of the animals with songs and dances.

After he had done this, Yuguk went to his parents' home. They had feared he would never return, and were overjoyed to have him safe at home again.

Yuguk did not make any more journeys. He stayed in the village and became a great hunter and whaling captain. After a

time he found himself a wife, and they had six children, three daughters and three sons.

Yuguk lived to be a very old man, honored in the village councils, and no one in the village ever knew he had once been a wooden doll.